A Life in Their Hands

Ramon Corujo
Illustrated by Dennis Balogh

STECK-VAUGHN
ELEMENTARY · SECONDARY · ADULT · LIBRARY

A Harcourt Company

www.steck-vaughn.com

Cover illustration by Alan Reingold

ISBN 0-7398-5100-4

Contents

Chapter 1

Too Cool for School

Manny Brito rode his bike fast. Too fast. He headed straight for John Lomatiwa.

Every school morning, John waited on his bike in front of his house. Manny rode to meet him. When Manny saw John, he raced right at him. At the last second, Manny always hit the brakes.

This time he'll crash into me for sure, John thought. He tried not to look worried.

Manny slammed on his brakes. He stopped just a few feet from John.

"Hey, John," Manny said, acting as if nothing had happened. "It's a cool day, right?"

"Right," John agreed.

Arizona is known for hot days. Summer is really hot. The temperature hits 110 degrees most days. It's too hot to do much outdoors.

Even in October, the temperature is often over 90. But today was different. It was 70 degrees and a nice day to be outdoors. It was also a school day.

"Too cool for school?" Manny asked.

Manny was daring John to skip school. John didn't really want to skip. He liked school more than Manny did. But it was a great day to be free. "Sure!" he said. "Too cool for school."

"Cool enough for hiking Little Peak trail?" Manny asked.

Another dare. John knew about the trail. It led up about a mile to the top of Little Peak Mountain.

The boys saw the mountain in the distance every day, but they had never hiked the trail. Other people said it was like climbing a mile-high stairway. It would be a challenge even on a cool day.

"No problem," John said. "I'm a rugged Hopi, remember?"

"I thought you were an American Indian," Manny said.

"Same thing," John answered. "I'm quick enough to beat you to the top."

"No way. I'll go up so fast, the trail will be renamed the Manny Brito Trail."

So the boys hit the trail, not the books. First they bought water. Then they rode to Little Peak. After an hour of tough biking, they arrived at the trail.

"See that post with the red phone? Let's lock our bikes there," Manny said.

"That's an emergency phone," John said. "It would be hard for someone to use the phone with bikes in the way." John worried about things like that.

"Like someone who sees kids skipping school?" Manny asked.

"Maybe," John laughed. "How about we just use that?" He pointed to a bike rack.

"My plan exactly," Manny said.

As the boys locked their bikes, they saw a warning sign.

```
┌────────────────────────────┐
│         DANGER!            │
│        Steep trail         │
│     People with heart or   │
│     breathing problems     │
│      should not climb.     │
└────────────────────────────┘
```

"You'd better not hike," Manny said, pointing to the sign.

John smiled. "My only problem will be laughing too hard when a paramedic has to help you down."

Manny chuckled. "We'll see who's laughing in an hour."

At first, the trail was easy. The boys started hiking quickly.

"This is nothing," Manny said.

John agreed. "It's like riding an escalator."

But the truth was a bit different. Both boys soon had sore legs and were soaked in sweat. Their walk slowed.

After twenty minutes, the boys spotted a stone bench.

"Want to sit?" asked Manny, who was breathing hard. He wasn't as tall as John. He had trouble keeping up with John's long stride.

"No way. I'm as fresh as the *piki* bread my mother made this morning," John answered between deep breaths. *Piki* is a special Hopi bread.

"Me, too," Manny gasped. "I just want to enjoy the view."

"Okay," John said quickly. "It's worth a look." Neither boy would admit he was tired.

The boys plopped down on the bench and drank some water. They caught their breath. The trail was almost empty. Then a strong-looking man hiked past and nodded hello.

After the man was gone, John asked, "Did you see the muscles on that guy? He's built like a wrestler."

Manny said, "Maybe he's in the WWF."

"The Little Peak Monster?" John joked.

The boys laughed. They were ready to hike again.

Chapter 2

A Real Emergency

The climb was harder now. The trail was much steeper and full of rocks. At last, the boys admitted they were tired.

"This trail is tougher than I thought," John puffed.

"I can't talk now," Manny puffed back. "I'm saving my breath for breathing."

The boys struggled up the trail. They stopped now and then to catch their breath, drink water, and give their tired muscles a rest. They also enjoyed the view. The higher they climbed, the better the view got.

They saw the tall buildings of the city. They saw planes take off from the airport. They even could see the new baseball park.

The boys stopped at another bench halfway up the mountain.

"This hard work is paying off," John said. "The view is great. I wish Mr. Atkins would take us here for a field trip." Mr. Atkins was one of the boys' teachers.

"That'll never happen," Manny said. "We'll be in big trouble if he finds out we were here today."

As they climbed even higher, the boys couldn't enjoy the view as much. They had to watch where they stepped. Small, sharp rocks poked through their shoes. Sometimes the boys had to scramble over large rocks on the trail. Twice, they found themselves close to the edge of the mountain. They could fall if they took one wrong step.

After almost forty-five minutes of climbing, John looked up. "There's the top," he gasped.

Manny looked up to the top and then at the path in front of them. "That's the top," he agreed. "But the trail ahead looks tougher than ever." Manny bent down to tie his shoe.

"We can do it," John said. He walked a few steps up the trail. "Hey, I see the wrestler by a bench not far ahead of us."

"Wow! We almost caught up with Mr. Muscles?" Manny asked in a surprised voice as he looked up. "I can't see him."

"I think he's waving to us," John said.

John started to wave back. Then he cried out, "Oh, no! He fell!"

Manny stood up. "Off the edge? I can't see him up there."

"No, not off the edge," John replied. "He's lying in front of the bench. I don't think he's moving."

The boys were frozen for a second. Then without a word, they raced uphill to the fallen hiker. They hustled over rocks and forgot about dangerous edges. They forgot that they were sore and tired.

They climbed the rough trail. The last few feet to the bench were the hardest.

Manny grabbed John's arm. "He looks dead. Is he breathing?"

John looked at the man. His body was twisted where he had fallen. His face was a scary, bluish gray.

"He's not breathing," John said. "I wonder if he had a heart attack."

Manny heard fear in John's voice. He felt fear in his own chest. "Call for help," Manny said.

"Help! Someone! Help!" the boys shouted louder and louder.

No one came.

"John, do you know CPR?" Manny asked. "That thing you do when you push on a person's chest."

The boys both looked at the man's face.

"No, I don't," John said. "I don't."

Manny shivered. He knew what he had to do. A few weeks ago, his mother had read him a newspaper story about a kind of CPR that was supposed to be easy to do. If you didn't have regular CPR training, you could use this way instead.

Manny's mom always worried about his dad's heart. She wanted everybody in the family to take first-aid classes. No one had done it yet. But she made sure Manny listened as she read the newspaper story. In fact, she read it to him twice.

"John," Manny said quickly. "I think I know what to do. Help me straighten him out."

John looked at Manny. "Okay," he whispered.

The man's body was heavy. His big muscles were hard to move when the man himself wasn't moving them.

"His body is warm," Manny said. "He must still be alive!"

"What are you going to do, Manny?" John asked.

Manny kneeled next to the chest of the fallen man. "I'm going to try a kind of CPR," he said.

Then he looked at John. "If you and I had raced up this mountain, you would have beaten me. You're fast. You're faster than anyone in school. Race down to the emergency phone and call for help. Run!"

John gave the man one more look, and then he was gone. ⚡

Chapter 3

Alone

Manny looked into the man's face. He knew that what he did next might mean life or death for this stranger.

He felt very alone. But then he heard his mother's voice reading the CPR story to him. "Kneel next to the patient." Manny was doing that.

"Draw an imaginary line across the patient's chest." Manny drew the imaginary line with his finger.

"Place the heel of one hand in the center of the line. Place the other hand on top of the first hand." He put his hands on the man's chest.

Is this right? he wondered. If it was, Manny knew his hands were just above the man's heart.

"Place your shoulders above the breastbone so that your arms go straight down to the breastbone." Manny was sure he had this right. Well, he was pretty sure.

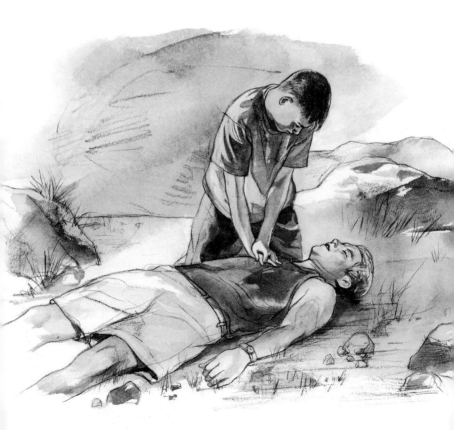

"Press down two inches or so. Then let up." He pushed on the man's chest. It was hard to do. *How do I know if I went two inches?* Manny thought. Then he screamed out loud, "Help! I need help!"

He heard his mother reading again. "Press down 15 times. Stop. Count up to two slowly. Then repeat the cycle." Manny counted carefully.

After 15 pushes, Manny stopped. The man didn't breathe. Manny felt tears in his eyes.

"Come on, mister, breathe. Please breathe," he said. He gave the man 15 more pushes. Then 15 more. Then 15 more, over and over. Soon Manny's hands, arms, and shoulders ached. But he didn't stop.

He's going to die, Manny thought. *I can't save him.* Manny had never felt so helpless. This powerful man's life was in his hands.

He tried to hear his mother's voice again. But there were no more directions. Manny thought about his father. Could he save his father if he had to? Could he save this man?

As Manny pumped the man's chest, he looked at the man's face. He hoped to see some sign of life. "Breathe, mister," he cried out loud again. "Please, please breathe!"

John didn't wait to see what Manny was going to do. He took off. At first, the run downhill was easier on his lungs than the climb up had been. But soon John was breathing hard again. He knew it was fear.

What if I don't get down there in time? he thought. *What if the man dies?*

Then John had a new fear. *How do I tell the paramedics where the man is?* he wondered. *What do I say?*

Then he remembered. The man fell at the third bench up on the Little Peak Trail. That's what he would tell the paramedics.

John ran on. Every now and then, his feet slipped on loose rocks. *What if the emergency phone doesn't work?* he worried. His thoughts raced. *I'll run farther then, to a nearby house or something.*

John was running faster and faster, but he felt slow. *I'm not moving fast enough,* he told himself. *I feel like the last bit of syrup dripping out of a bottle.*

Suddenly, he realized that the trail looked different. Was he lost? Had he taken a wrong turn?

Then he saw a familiar group of trees. He just had to keep going down, straight down to the phone.

Lost in his fears, John soon lost his footing. He fell forward, hit his knees and his hands, and then hit his head hard on a rock.

Back up the trail, Manny continued the cycle. Pump the man's chest 15 times, stop, count to two, start again. His arms and shoulders almost screamed with pain. *I hope John made it to the phone,* he thought. *I hope help is on the way.*

Manny was so busy giving CPR that he didn't notice two hikers walking down the trail toward him. They had been to the top of Little Peak. Now they were hiking back down.

"Look at that boy!" the man said. "He's doing CPR on someone!"

The woman took a deep breath. "Jeff, use the cell phone to call the paramedics. I'm going down to help him," she said.

Manny heard her footsteps as she ran toward him. He looked up at her face but kept pushing the fallen man's chest. "Please, help me," he said. His voice was weak. His arms and chest were weak.

The woman kneeled beside the man. "What's your name?" she asked.

"Manny."

"Manny, my name's Nikki Tate. I'm a nurse. My husband, Jeff, is calling for help on our cell phone," she said.

"A nurse!" Manny said with surprise and relief.

"Is this man your father?" she asked.

"No, I don't know who he is," Manny said.

Nikki quickly put her fingers in the man's mouth to see if anything was blocking his breathing. It was clear.

Next, she dug in her backpack and found an empty plastic sandwich bag. She made a little hole in it and put it over the man's mouth.

"Manny, I know you're tired. Rest for a moment," Nikki said.

She lifted the man's head a bit and kept one hand under his neck. With the other hand, Nikki squeezed his nose shut. She leaned forward, took a deep breath, and put her mouth on the plastic that covered the man's mouth.

Then she blew into it. When she did, her breath passed through the hole in the plastic bag and into the man. His chest rose.

Manny's eyes got bigger. "He's moving. He's alive!" he shouted.

A male voice said, "Maybe, but his chest only rose because my wife blew air into it." It was Jeff, Nikki's husband.

"Help is on the way," he added. "Let me take over for you." Manny moved aside.

Jeff kneeled in Manny's place and started doing chest pushes on the victim, just as Manny had. Nikki continued blowing air into the man's mouth. Manny watched as the wife-and-husband team worked. "Please save him," he said softly.

Chapter 4

Dead or Alive?

John pulled himself up from where he had fallen. His head was bleeding, and he was a little dizzy, but he got up and started to run again. *Hopis have run up and down Arizona mountains for more than a thousand years,* he thought. *I can do this faster.*

He ran as fast as he could. He jumped over rocks and bushes. When he saw a turn in the trail, he made an instant shortcut, cutting over rough ground.

Faster, faster, he told himself over and over.

Sweat and blood ran into his eyes. He couldn't see the trail for a second or two, but that didn't slow him.

Finally, the trail got wider. He knew he was near the bottom at last.

John spotted the phone. He rushed to pick it up. Right away he heard a woman's voice saying, "Park Emergency Line. Can I help you?"

"A man is dying!" John yelled into the phone. "Please send help. Please!" 🎵

"Try to calm down. Tell me slowly what happened, and we'll send help," the woman said.

John gave the woman all the important facts. Then he sat down on a nearby picnic table. He was very tired. *I'll wait here for the paramedics. I'll lead them up,* he thought.

Then he noticed that his knees, hands, and head were bleeding. He didn't care. He just wanted the man to live. 🎵

A minute or two after he sat down, he heard a siren. An ambulance was pulling up at the foot of the trail.

As two paramedics got out, John jumped off the picnic table. "He's up there! I'll lead you up," he yelled and pointed up the trail.

One paramedic took a look at his cuts. "No, son," he said calmly. "You stay down here with my partner. I'll go up to the victim."

The paramedic looked strong and healthy. John knew he would make it up the trail in no time. But then he thought, *Mr. Muscles looked strong and healthy, too. I can't believe we called him that.*

The paramedic put a backpack of first-aid equipment over his shoulder and started running up the trail. The other paramedic made a radio call and then said to John, "Young man, sit back down on that picnic table. You need a little first aid."

While the paramedic cleaned John's cuts, John said to her, "I can't believe you got here so fast. I just made the call on that emergency phone."

"Your call was reported to us," said the paramedic. "But we were already on the way. Someone on the trail made a call from a cell phone."

John felt strange. Of course, he was glad that an earlier call had been made. That meant the paramedics had arrived sooner and maybe they could save the man. It also meant that someone on the trail was helping Manny. But John felt as if he had failed. He was too slow. He should have run faster.

Up on the trail, Nikki and Jeff worked on the man. There was no sign of life yet. Manny watched them. He heard a noise on the trail below. He looked down and saw a paramedic running steadily toward them. Manny stood and yelled, "Here! We're here!"

The paramedic raced the last few yards to the bench, scrambling up the trail as John and Manny had earlier. Once there, he quickly took some first-aid equipment out of his backpack. While the paramedic took a good look at the victim, Nikki and Jeff kept working to save him.

"My wife is a nurse," Jeff said.

"Good," said the paramedic. "She can stay up here with me." He looked at Manny and added, "But will you take this young man down the trail to my partner?"

Manny and Jeff were halfway down when they heard the sound of a helicopter growing louder and closer.

In seconds, the helicopter was nearby. It was landing somewhere on the mountain above them. They couldn't see where.

"They'll take the man to a hospital," said Jeff. "There are a couple of helicopter landing pads on Little Peak."

When Manny looked surprised, Jeff added, "Emergencies happen a lot here."

"I hope he makes it," Manny said sadly.

Jeff gave Manny a pat on the shoulder. "Me, too," he said.

About twenty minutes later, Manny and Jeff got to the bottom of the trail. John grabbed Manny's arm and asked, "Is he okay? Is the man okay?"

"We don't know yet," Manny answered.

"What happened to your head?"

"Nothing," said John.

While Jeff talked quietly to the paramedic at the ambulance, the boys sat on the picnic table. After a few minutes, they heard the helicopter. They saw it racing across the sky.

"He'll be in a hospital soon," Manny said.

The boys didn't have to say any more. Each knew what the other felt. Fear. Fear that they had failed. Fear that the man was dead.

It seemed that they waited for hours, but only thirty minutes later the paramedic's radio crackled with sound. The boys listened carefully.

A man's voice said, "Williams, this is Smith. The victim was a man named Carl Davis. He arrived at the hospital DOA. Please return to the station."

"Who was that?" John asked.

"My partner," the paramedic answered.

"What does DOA mean?" Manny asked. He was pretty sure he knew.

The paramedic stood in front of the boys. "I'm sorry. We couldn't save him," she said. "DOA means that Mr. Davis was dead on arrival at the hospital."

Chapter 5

A Visitor

It was Tuesday that the boys had skipped school. It was Tuesday that they had climbed Little Peak. It was Tuesday that the stranger had died on the trail.

On Wednesday, Manny missed school again. This time he was sick. He couldn't sleep or eat. His stomach was in a knot. He couldn't think about anything except what had happened and how he had failed.

John went to school on Wednesday. He had to. He had to stay busy. He didn't want to think about Tuesday ever again. He didn't want to remember that if he had run faster, a dead man might be alive.

On Thursday, Manny's mom and dad made him go to school. Even though he sat next to John in Mr. Atkins's class, they didn't talk to each other. They barely even looked at each other.

The boys did share time in detention after school. After what had happened, there was no way to hide that they had skipped school. So they had to sit for an hour after school each day for the next two weeks.

It was in detention that Mr. Atkins found them.

"Boys, there are two women here to see you, a nurse named Nikki Tate and a woman named Mrs. Davis," he said.

The boys looked at each other. Mrs. Davis must be Carl Davis's wife.

"Oh, no, Manny!" John said. "She's going to blame us."

Manny looked at John and then at his teacher. "I've thought about it a lot. I know we did the very best we could," he said. "But part of me knows we didn't do enough. Do we have to see her?"

Mr. Atkins was silent for a moment. "I called you boys when I walked in here. I should have called you men. Although it wasn't right to skip school, you were adults on that mountain. You were brave and smart."

39

Then he paused before saying, "Men, you can do this next thing easily."

The boys looked at each other. Manny nodded to John. They followed Mr. Atkins to Mrs. Davis and Nikki.

When they walked into the office, Nikki said, "Manny, John, this is Mrs. Davis. She has something to tell you."

The boys waited for Mrs. Davis to speak. It was clear she'd been crying.

"Thank you for seeing me. I know this is hard for you," she said. "I do have something to tell you. But first I want to tell you about my husband." ⚡

The boys were puzzled.

"Carl was a strong man. He had a strong body and a strong mind," Mrs. Davis said.

"We thought he looked liked a wrestler," John said quietly. Manny frowned.

"Carl would be happy to hear you say that," Mrs. Davis said with a sad smile. "The only thing that wasn't strong about Carl was his heart. Before Tuesday, he'd already had two heart attacks."

Manny wasn't sure he should ask the next question, but he did. "Then why did he climb Little Peak?"

"He wanted to live life to the fullest," she said. "It was right for him. So while Carl was here in Arizona on business, he decided to go on a hike."

She added, "The heart attack might have happened if he had stayed in his hotel. Instead, he did what he enjoyed. That was Carl." Her eyes filled with tears.

Manny and John did not know what to say. Nikki did.

"Manny, the doctors say that Mr. Davis was dead before you started CPR," she said.

Manny was silent. He put his head down.

"That's right," said Mrs. Davis. "But Nikki saw you give him CPR. She said you did it exactly right."

Manny's eyes burned. Mrs. Davis gently put her hand on his arm. "Manny, you couldn't save him. No one could have saved him. But you tried your best, and that's what's important."

Then she looked at John.

"And John, the park rangers told me something amazing. My husband's watch broke when he fell. So we know what time he died."

She swallowed. It was hard for her to talk.

"The Park Emergency Line knows what time you phoned for help," she said after a moment. "When the rangers at Little Peak checked the two times, they were shocked. You ran down most of the trail as fast as anybody ever has. If you had run that fast from the very top, you might have set a new record."

"But it wasn't fast enough," said John.

"Yes, it was," Mrs. Davis said. "It was an amazing effort to save a life."

The boys were both sniffling a little.

"You should have been in school on Tuesday," Mrs. Davis said quietly.

Manny agreed. "We know. We've learned our lesson."

John nodded.

Mrs. Davis continued, "But I feel lucky that you were on the trail. That's why I'm here. You're both heroes. You need to know that. If it had been possible to save Carl's life, you two would have done it. I thank you for trying so very, very hard."

She gave each boy a hug.

"I know that thinking about Carl's death will be hard for you," she said. "But you gave him your best."

As Mrs. Davis walked away, the boys were silent. Finally Manny cleared his throat. "Thank you, Mrs. Davis," he said.

"Yes," added John. "We're glad you came here."

Mrs. Davis turned to the boys. "I'm glad you were there."